The Ominous Dragoon of Dothdura

STORYTELLER
Ramtha, The Enlightened One
MASTERSCRIBE
Douglas James Mahr
ILLUSTRATOR EXTRAORDINAIRE
Jerry Banghart

FIRST EDITION
MASTERWORKS, INC.
Publishers

The Ominous Dragoon of Dothdura

Copyright©1985 by **MASTERWORKS, INC.**

All rights reserved. No part of this book may be reproduced or transmitted in any form or by any means, electronic or mechanical, including photocopying, recording, or by any information storage or retrieval system, without permission in writing from the Publisher. This work is based, in part, upon Ramtha Dialogues®, a series of magnetic recordings authored by J. Z. Knight, with her permission.

MASTERWORKS, INC.
Publishers

Post Office Box 901
Friday Harbor, Washington 98250

First Edition, First Printing—1985

Book design by Mitzi Johnson,
Art Director of Masterworks

Library of Congress Cataloging in Publication Data

Ramtha, the enlightened one.
    The ominous dragoon of Dothdura.

    Based on magnetic recordings authored by J. Z. Knight.
    Summary: Relates how Prince Gallant saves a village enslaved by a ferocious "Dragoon."
    1. Children's stories, American. [1. Fairy tales]
I. Mahr, Douglas James, 1946- . II. Banghart, Jerry, ill. III. Knight, J. Z. (Judy Zebra) IV. Title. PZ8.R150m 1985   [Fic]   84-62175
ISBN 0-931317-13-4

PRINTED IN UNITED STATES OF AMERICA

ILLUSTRATIONS

The Hands of the Storyteller   6
The Frightened Village   8
The Gallant Prince Arrives   10
His Short Sword & Scabbard   12
The Prince Takes a Home in Princely Style   13
The "Dragoon" Rumbles   15
Prince Gallant Faces Dothdura   16
Spinning the Tale of the Dragoon   19
The Prince Dons His Armor   21
Our Prince in the Dust   23
The Townsfolk Assist Their "Hero"   25
A "Farewell" Bid to Their Prince   26
The Noble Steed Has Other Ideas   29
Calling the Dragoon Out To Do Battle   31
Into the Dragoon's Lair   33
Our Hero Staggers!   35
Our Prince Faces His Challenge   37
The Moment of Conquest   39
Our Prince Returns Triumphant!   42
The Victory Celebration   45
The Joy of the Children   46

DEDICATION
To Brooks

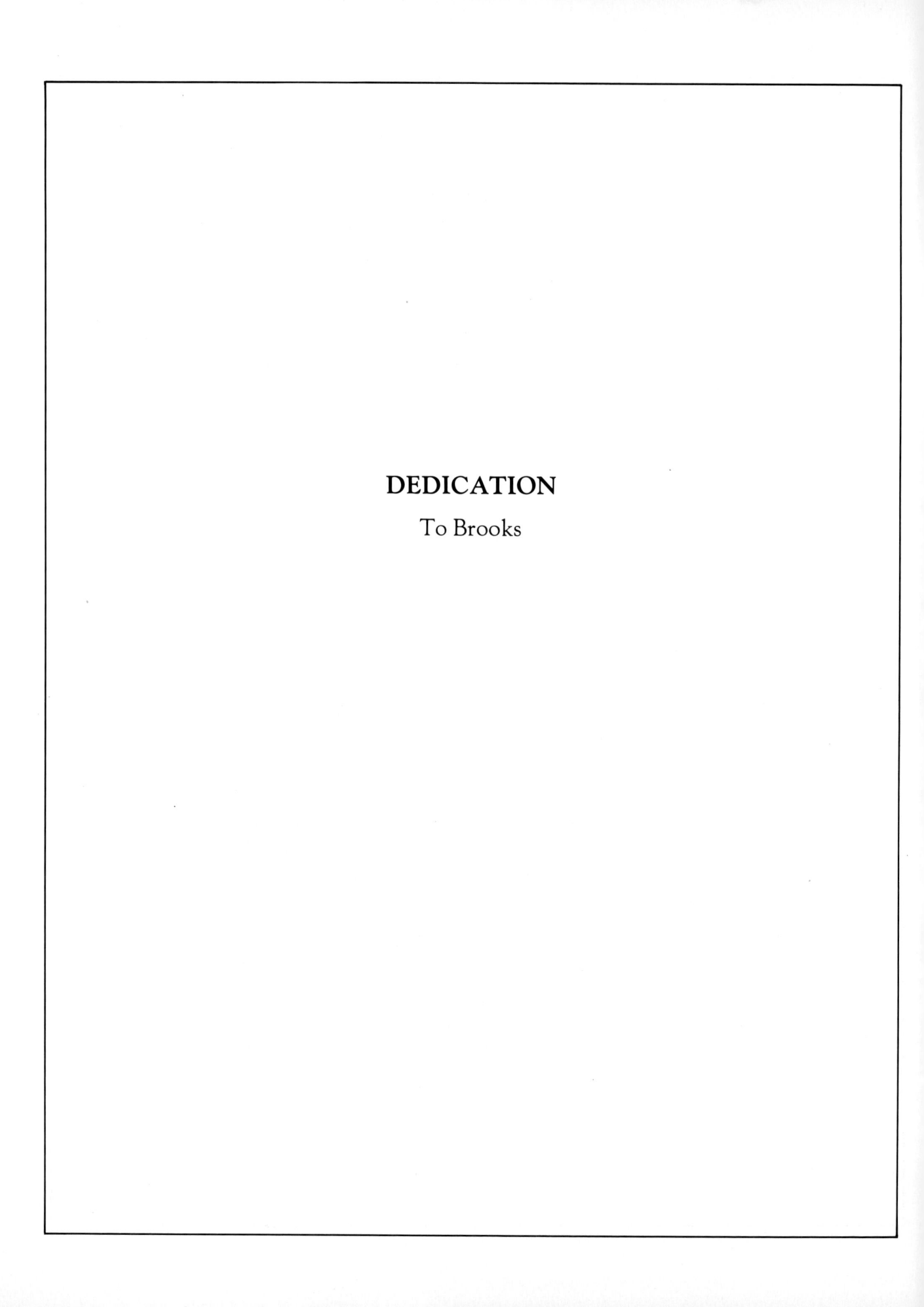

READER, PLEASE NOTE:

THIS STORY, *The Ominous Dragoon of Dothdura*, as expressed herein, is *not* the verbatim story as it was imparted by Ramtha, The Enlightened One. Some of Ramtha's words and phrases, particularly, "as it were indeed," "indeed," "that which is termed," were deleted by the Masterscribe. You will note that Ramtha occasionally speaks a sentence both in the present and the past tense.

You will also notice a few unusual usages, for instance the word "bane." In all instances, words not known or used rarely in the 20th century were searched for meaning. Those words discovered while searching various dictionaries were left intact. Some words not found in these dictionaries were deleted. We have assumed that the usage of these words was common in the time that this story unfolded, yet the continuation of the meaning was not passed forward in the generations to come. Some of these words without contemporary definition were left intact if they did not distract, in our opinion, from the unfoldment of the scene.

Communication in the 1980's is visually oriented. Therefore, the scenes constructed by the Masterscribe in this work were visually oriented to place the reader *in* the scene. To assist in creating these visualizations, the Masterscribe utilized writing techniques and devices common today which consequently expanded and embellished some of the Ramthinian scenes herein.

In summary, the majority of the words which comprise the story, *The Ominous Dragoon of Dothdura* are those of Ramtha, The Enlightened One. This story, as presented herein, is a derivative work based upon the writings of J. Z. Knight and developed from the complete story as it was imparted by Ramtha.

YOU ARE a young Master of sorts, are you not? Young Masters who try to understand a *seen* world that has outgrown them, do find in their *dream* world a smaller and more truthful place of comfort, for it is easy to understand accomplishments of their very dreams. Let me tell you of an accomplishment, Master, in your dreams, in *your* world, that greater people called adults, as they are so seen in their world, have long forgotten and remember no more. Listen to me—there is a good story I wish you to partake of, Master, at your own permission of course, to add to the world of all who have outgrown their childhood. Listen to me.

There once was a mountain called Dothdura. This mountain, it was magnificently beautiful, yet ominous at the same moment. When Dothdura was peaceful in the essence of its being, all life shimmered in its calm. When Dothdura was angry in the pits of its being, the skyline belched with dark and ominous purple and black smoke! And all the people of the land who sat under the cool, soothing shade of the great mountain while it was peaceful, ran inside their houses and shut their windows and their doors and locked themselves in what is termed cellars when Dothdura was angry, for great fear comes from this place. A mountain, a meager mountain has caused such fear in the land? What an atrocity!

There comes forth from the river that is called Samida a beautiful entity. The entity was a young man of some renown and stature in being and purpose, who had come to this place from a far land to make his home under the mountain. The entity is obviously a prince, for princes have an astute air about them—wherever they go, people have small tendencies of bowing before them. So, we shall readily assume that this small prince of sorts who came into the land was what was called "divine" in his might. Let us find the name. Oh! Let us find the name indeed, and find it not the name of *every* day. We shall call him indeed "gallant." Ah, Prince Gallant . . . most remarkable name.

Let me describe this beautiful prince that has come from a far place. He has upon the crown of his being great and golden locks that flowed freely about his divine shoulders. Within his eyes is a cerulean blueness—the countenance in their beauty, one can be lost in them. His face—'twas firm and his jaw line permanent, but no hair sit upon it thus giving readily to the image that the prince be young. Upon his mouth was a great and glorious smile to all things that he saw. Ah . . . as I see him now, the air of snobbery that was linked to him was mighty. Thus, *you* are a mighty snob called Prince Gallant!

This entity came upon the shores of the land not knowing of its captivity to the Mountain Dothdura. Yet, as he embarked unto this land foreign to him, he readily braced his hand upon his short sword ('twas a small gift from his father).

In time, our "prince" secured what is called a home under the Great Mountain. There he began to live his life in a princely sort of way.

And behold, there came a great and ominous fear! And all the people went scurrying about. And all the handmaidens that tended and flattered the gallant prince as it were, all went running from his eminence. He commanded that they all cease fluttering and flapping and come to him. And no one listened! With all the fit and trauma that he did pour out from his being, he was not happy for no one obeyed him. And soon the very floor that the prince stood upon began to rumble beneath him. "Hmmmmmmm," he wondered to himself.

And the young prince unsteadily walks onto what is called the streetway of his place and what does he see within the sky? Lo, where are the doves that were once up there this morning? And where is the sun in its ceaseless journey to come to and fro across the sky? And what was this murk and mire and muck that was in the heavens? Where was it coming from?

The young prince rubbed his eyes for the stuff burned them. With one eye tearing and the other painfully shut tight, he peered at the mountain where all this belching was coming from. "Hmmmmmmmm . . . ," a rotten sort of feeling to be standing there all alone when all others are hiding. The prince sat himself down and looked upon the mountain and watched it roar. The sky became darker and more ominous. He looked around at all the streets and at what was once the busy market place—'twas all shut up tight! There wasn't even a yelping as it were, of a small dog to be heard! And the prince stared at the mountain.

Soon the rumbling ceased. In the moment of its ceasement, the dark cloud menaced its "good-day" and passed from the shadow of the land, the sky peeked through and delicately returned to blue, and the birds ventured cautiously from their nests and began their daily and morning vigil of singing and being busy-bodies. Behold—one by one, all the village doors begin to open and peeking heads begin to peer out and business as usual is commenced in the market place. And the prince was most bemused by this action.

He went unto his handmaidens and he commands, "I charge you, pray tell, to tell me about this mountain!" And they all shivered when he asked them about the mountain, and they whimpered unto him, "Oh, Master and Lord, there is a great evil that lives in this mountain! And though we do not know when it will come upon the land, it is sheer terror when it comes forth. We bane and we are fearful for our lives!" The small prince articulated, "Then I *command* you to tell me who makes this fearful thing?" They said, " 'Tis a great *Dragoon* who lives at the bottom of the mountain. And when he becomes angry and hungry he begins to belch and snort and all the smoke comes forth, and we are surely terrified, for our lives and our children's, that the Dragoon will come down and partake of the entire village!" And they all shrieked, "And we are *most* fearful!" And the prince mused, "Dragoon? In the mountain? And I charge you to tell me what a *dragoon* is?" Well, I wish you to know that *all* the little women stammered in quivering horror, "Dragoon! Oh! Master . . . Lord, it is a most ominous creature. OH! It is snake-like, and has great nostrils and breathes terrible fire, and its tail . . . Oh! When its tail pounds the earth we *all* shiver. And when you see the billowing smoke come out, it is the Dragoon calling for his supper . . . "

"Dragoon indeed," scoffed the prince.

Well, I wish you to know that the little prince, not wishing to be outdone and not wishing to be fearful of any *one* or any *thing*, pronounced that *he* would sear the Dragoon! All begin to weep, for surely in their hearts they felt that their prince would become the supper of the Dragoon who lives in the great mouth of Dothdura!

The little prince called Gallant, being snobbish in his air, marched off gallantly to his dressing chamber. He called forth there his handmaiden to assist him in readying for this battle. He put on his greatest mail, and this mail was of raw silver. And thence, the protective plates of armor were carefully, tenderly fitted over his princely beingness. He purveyed the fit, flexing his arms occasionally, mind you, to ensure their mobility during the battle. And in that moment he perceived himself as the conquering hero, and we suppose he was to be. His handmaiden bowed to her image of holiness. She presented him with helmet of silvered bronze crowned with its plume of forest green that would ride with the wind.

And lo, the villagers brought forth the fastest steed in the land. The steed, as it were, was a poor wretched creature of some renown who had seen better days. Now, the prince, such as he was and after much *to do*, began to mount his steed. With one foot firmly in the appropriate stirrup, he thrust himself up with the essence of his might. Quite unfortunately however, his thrust of energy missed its target (that being the saddle) and collided with the side of the beast. So heavily burdened was he, that he, quite unheroically, collapsed into a clanking pile of dust! Very befitting of princely drama, aye?

Have you ever clothed your body with a coat of armor? Then you would know the humbleness our hero felt in this moment, for there he lay, without fanfare, flat on his back. He could not move save for his arms and legs, clinking and clanking they were as they waved in the air quite helplessly. I am sure, were we able to observe the countenance of Prince Gallant, it would have blushed toward the color crimson. Yet, at his moment of impact with the earth, his visor has slammed shut upon him! This was for good purpose for he was unable to view the thin smiles of those who approached to aid their prince.

Those townsfolk who had gathered glanced at one another through nervous smiles. I surely don't wish blame upon them—their prince, who was to save them from the wrath of the Dragoon of Dothdura, has been conquered by his own armor! Quite an unfortunate scene to behold, indeed. Well, a few of the townsfolk joined together to put forth a stool. They lifted their prince up from his ponderous pile of dust and righted him. His visor remained clanked shut which hid from them the articulation of his princely expression.

When the young prince managed to force open his visor, he found himself mounted upon this not-so-hearty horse ready to make battle with the great fear in the land—the Great Dragoon of Dothdura! And away they made with banners flying and trumpets blaring, on to the great mountain to slay the Dragoon. Hmmmm . . . well lo, I wish to tell you, Master, heartily here and now, that all saluted him. And women with their kerchiefs were blowing their kisses and wiping their tears, and wiser men were shaking their heads, and children were laughing and screaming to see the young prince go for the Dragoon.

And soon, as it was in his time, the shouts and the weeping and the crying became softer and softer in his ears until all he could hear was the climpity-clomp of his steed of "renown" and the approach of the song birds bringing forth the evening. And it was this Prince Gallant who alone rode. And they climpity-clomped along, and his visor continually kept flopping shut so he could not see where he was nor where he went. And he kept flipping this obnoxious lid open, and it kept banging shut without respect to his princeliness. And he lifted it, and it clanked shut, and he flung it open, and it clanked shut, and this continued with consistency until his steed lurched to an abrupt halt. He held his visor full open . . . and what his eyes beheld was the ominous mountain of Dothdura! And for a brief instant, the menace of fear crept into his bones. But this *fear* was unprincely to him, so be banished it from the Kingdom of His Being forever more. For it was this prince who had promised to slay the Great Dragoon of Dothdura, and he had promised to do so regardless of the twinge of doubt in his gut.

So, without further embarrassment to his pride, he rode ceaselessly into the night 'til early morning was at the crest of the mountain. The prince was soon to find that his courage had not rubbed off on others who were near. His steed, after now having considerable time to discover where he was carrying the prince of the land, decided that he did not wish to clomp nor clack any further (perhaps a wise decision)!

Prince Gallant removed his princeliness from this "traitor" and cursed and spat upon him calling him a "useless nag," while said "useless nag" proceeded to munch upon that which was nearby that was munchable. Our prince put himself upon the ground, falling once. Soon, with great difficulty (and the help of a nearby tree), he managed to pull himself up from the dirt and dust. He left his nag to his nibbling and began the march up the abandoned passageway that ended, almost too suddenly, at the terrible door of the Mountain of Dothdura.

Well, I wish you to know right here and now that the prince drew his short sword with great aplomb, stood up most erect, and stalked and clinked and clanked into the mouth of this mountain of mystery and intrigue. And, in an instant, his arrogant stalking and ponderous clanking became the wisdom of a pause . . . for he was forced to peer into the vastness of an eerie blackness! He heard a thought of his, "Hmmm, this could be worse than I thought at first!" He began to study the immensity of the challenge of this endless, bottomless pit.

He moved onward, with caution . . .

His nostrils began to flare as the hideous odor of Dragoon intimidated them. Then puffs, and then *clouds* of smoke belched up from the darkness of nowhere and reddened his eyes until his tears blinded his sight. And the little boy, sniffing and fuming and wiping his eyes while he blinked, trying to see beyond his tears, heard an awful rumbling underneath him. He stared down into the blackness, "Dragoon . . . DRAGOON! I order you to come forth to do battle with the true Lord of this land! I order you, NOW!" And our little prince, preparing for battle, fiddled and fumbled, clinking and clanking with the ponderousness of his armor. Then, brandishing his short sword he was at last all erect . . . and nothing came forth!

Prince Gallant, not wishing to be laughed at, spoke it forth again, this time a bit louder, "CURSE YOU, DRAGOON! COME OUT AND FIGHT LIKE A MAN, OR A DRAGON, OR WHATEVER YOU ARE!" Our little prince was most perplexed. There was no answer at all.

Determined not to return to the townsfolk as a defeated, unconquering hero, Prince Gallant began to search for passageways to storm this impervious mountain. Quite surely he came upon a not-so-steep incline. He traversed down passage by passage, footstep over carefully placed footstep, and heard far echoings of strange sounds, and lizards hissing in his ear. He was determined, as it were indeed, to *not* be defeated!

"Hmmmm . . . the river that burns . . ."

A low rumbling intruded into his thought. The wall he was grasping onto began to move and shake. Rocks began to pour into this place. Boulders crashed against one another, some pommeling off his armor, clanking his eardrums into a state of deafness. This avalanche, of sorts, roared for a brief time while boulders of destruction ground themselves into pebbles. Splinters were a-flying amidst the uproar of dust clouded against the ominous orange glow of this River of Fire. A sliver grazed the cheek of our young hero, and he took it like a man. And as soon as he did so, Master, he realized that the Dragoon that all had feared was not a *dragon* at all—'twas a mountain with a bellyache! Hmmmm. Well, it *was* of some small relief to the young prince that there was not a dragon that would require slaying but truly that the mountain burned, quaked and ached! Thus, the little prince looked about him, with his head in an enviable tilt. Then, summoning all of his reclaimed fearlessness, he spat into the Lake of Fire. He spat within the lake, cursing it . . .

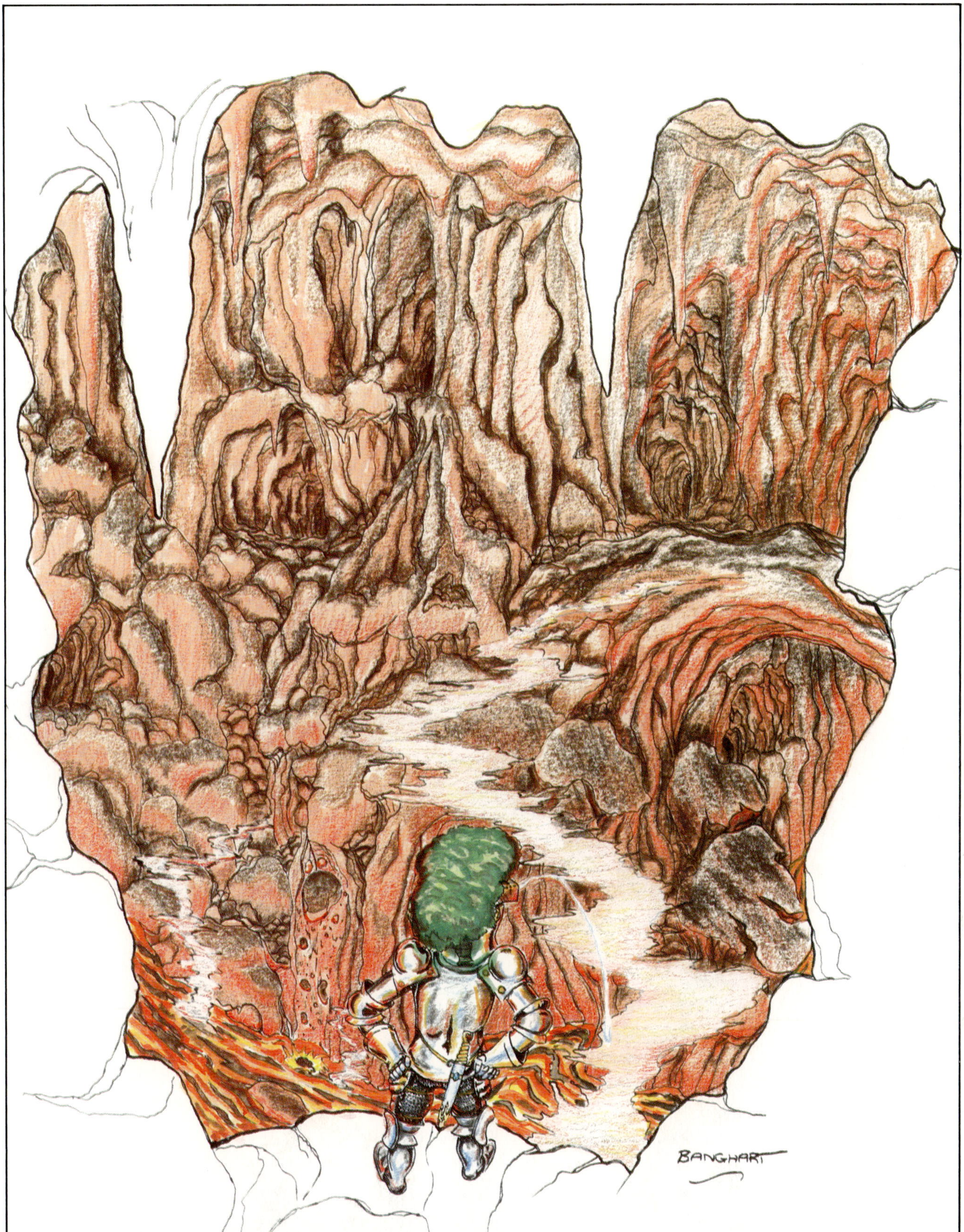
BANGHART

. . . and it froze immediately!

    The little prince hearkened unto this crackling and cracking of the waters as they formed beautiful mirrors of reflective strength in patterns of intertwined lace. His eyes soon saw that all was pleasantly frozen. There was no more searing heat nor billowing sulphur that, in a past of a moment ago, inflamed the eye and intimidated the Soul. This once frightening spectacle has crystallized into a beautiful mountain that no longer belly-ached nor belched! And he saw what was once ominous and forbidden now shimmering in its own reflective beauty.

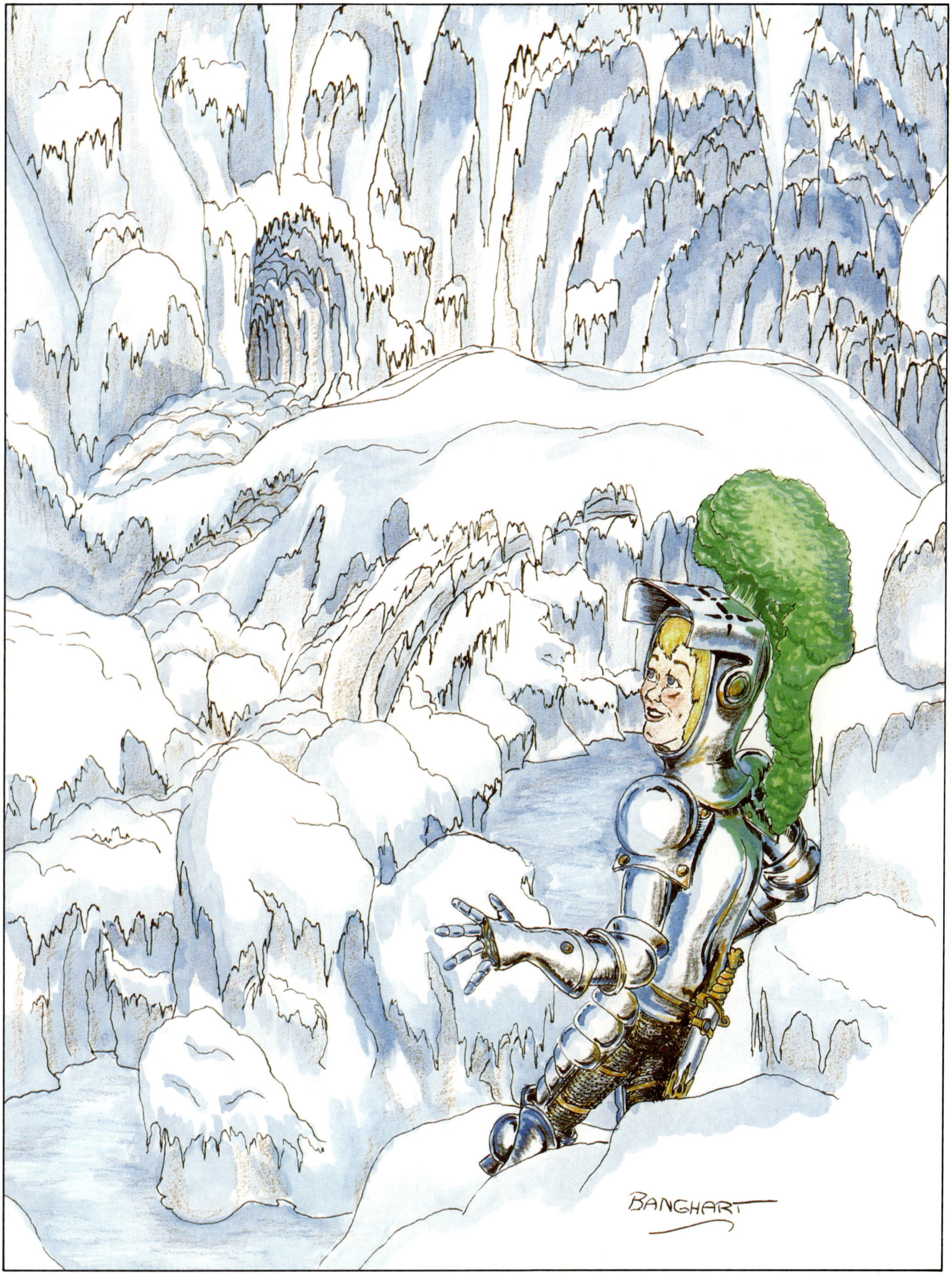
BANGHART

Well, I wish you to know, our hero prince, gathering up all of his glory, was to return unto his tiny kingdom very joyous that he had spit in the eye of the Dragoon and froze him into eternity. Thus, he collected himself, clinking and clacking with the weight of his armor upon his body, yet now it felt to him a bit lighter. And slipping as it were, but always regaining his balance, he climbed upward from his arena of triumph.

Slowly, with diligence, he came unto the crevasse to which he had called forth the Dragoon. He stood himself erect and reviewed the land as a king would. Ah! Good has been done by he! He has spit in the eye of the Dragoon and froze him for forever. And now peace was returning to his Princedom. Ah . . . the pleasures of conquering heroes! The small prince climbed out from the crevasse of his challenge into the light of his new world and was soon to discover his friend, the poor wretched beast, nibbling on some insignificant grass fairly oblivious to *all* that had gone on. Some things never change, aye!

And Prince Gallant attempted to mount his wretched steed — three times failing miserably, the fourth time succeeding. At the least, he has learned not to rely on the townsfolk for a remount! And now, quite settled and content in his saddle, he paraded gallantly toward his village. And all awaited his return . . .

His villagers could hear his approach as he clipped and clomped and clanked toward them. To his chagrin, his villainous visor clanked down tight upon him — the townsfolk could not observe the glow from his smile that would have proclaimed to them, "Victory!" Yet, they knew something joyous was on the wind, for his steed meandered forth with a bit more fanciful gait.

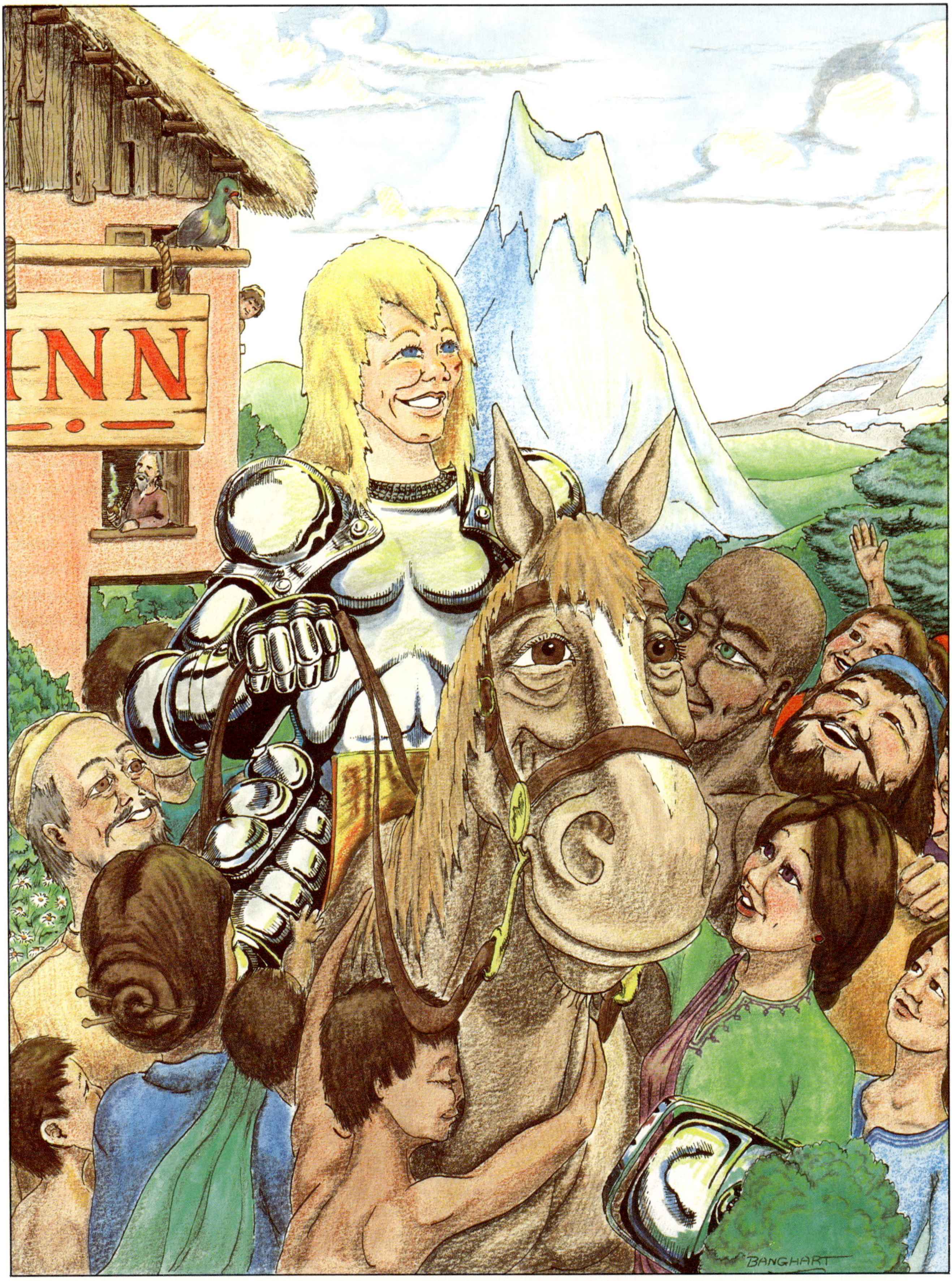
NN
BANGHART

Prince Gallant had returned! The villagers swarmed out from their hovels to surround their prince. His steed pranced about in one spot. They awaited in wild anticipation of the news. He raised his visor in salute to his conquered and then he was pleased to proclaim, "I have gone into the depths of the House of the Dragoon. I have met him on his own terms. I have done battle with him justly, as a man does. I have spit in his eye. And when I spit in his eye, he no longer is. He has become frozen!"

Well, all the townsfolk broke out into ecstatic jubilation! Children laughed and screamed with glee, and geese were scattering all about squeaking and squawking. And men, as it were indeed, passed around to all drafting ales and beer, and drinking to the health of the gallant prince began. And the women were falling all about him.

45

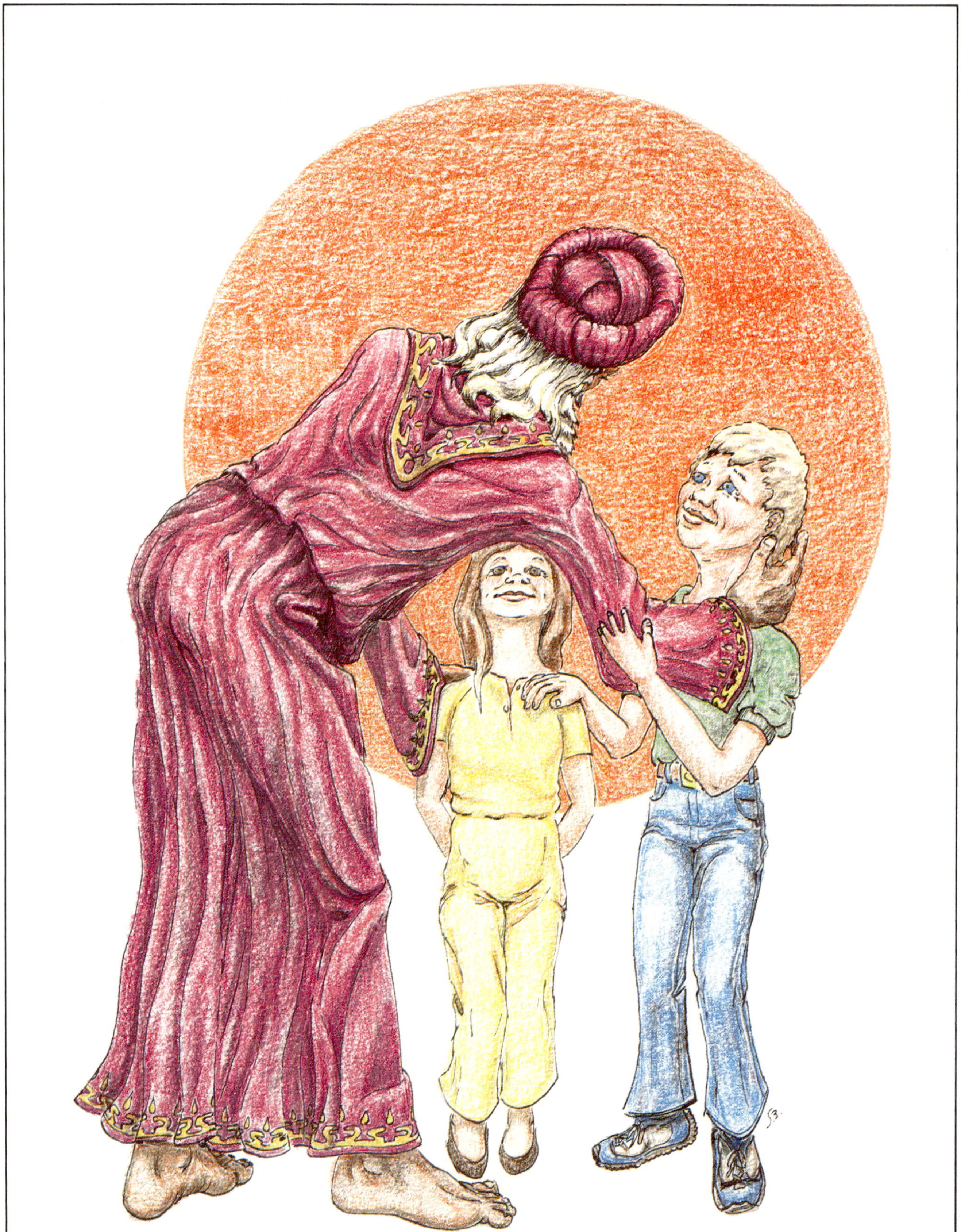

Am I Not a Good Spinner of Tales?

'Tis so good to be a hero, Master, when in these times there are none. 'Tis so good to be the leader who conquers fear when no one else will. You see, *you* were such a prince in such a place. But it was not a dragon that you conquered, it was the *fear* that gripped the land. You were one entity who exposed the fear. And all who lived in their peaceful villages truly did live in what is termed "happily ever after."

You see, dreams—they *do* come true. You were such an entity and conquered fear you did! You are pleased? Am I not a good spinner of tales? Wondrous entity, you will be one who will grow up and become a justly entity. Of all the good you shall deliver to this plane, the greatest good of all, Master, is that you live your truth in your life in spite of others' fears and fallacies. And you will not know fear for you will learn to look fear in the eye. For when you look fear in the eye, precious entity, the fear that you feel *will* disappear.

The End